Going Turbo

by Dan Danko and Tom Mason
Based on the teleplay "Strangers" written by Greg Weisman

SCHOLASTIC INC.
New York Toronto London Auckland Sydney
Mexico City New Delhi Hong Kong Buenos Aires

ISBN 0-439-22561-2

12 11 10 9 8 7 6 5 4 3 2   1 2 3 4 5 6/0

Printed in the U.S.A.
First Scholastic printing, December 2001

Chapter

1

"I hate this!"

Josh McGrath was bored. He had been reading his history book for two hours, although now it was more staring than reading. He read on his back, rolled over to his stomach, read at the desk, and then tried the couch. But no matter where or how Josh sat, he could not alter one inescapable fact: He was bored.

How could he not be? Josh's extreme-sports abilities were what got his adrenaline flowing, not studying. Still, even though he looked like a typical jock, nineteen-year-old Josh was definitely more brains than brawn — despite his failed encounter with his U.S. history book.

He flipped the book closed. *U.S. History Since the Civil War* would just have to wait for another night. Josh rolled over on the couch and grabbed the TV remote. With a push of the button, the silent black box sprung to life and flashed images before Josh's eyes.

"Man," he said, flipping through the stations like he was in a race. "Two hundred channels and not a single *Gilligan's Island* episode?"

Josh turned off the TV and tossed the remote on the couch. It was official. He was desperate. Unless he found something, anything to do, he'd have to study again — and there was no way he was going to let that happen.

Josh grabbed the phone and hit the auto-dial for his dad's cell phone. After a few rings, Jefferson Smith answered.

"Hey, Dad," Josh said to his father.

"Josh! Great to hear from you, Son," Jefferson greeted him happily. "Is everything okay?"

"Yeah, Dad. Fine." Josh sighed.

"So you need money, then?" Jefferson asked.

"No, Dad I — look, I know I haven't called you in a week —"

"Two."

"Two weeks," Josh continued, "but I was wondering if you'd like to have dinner tonight?"

"Nothing would make me happier," Jefferson said. Josh practically saw him smiling through the phone. "I'll meet you outside N-Tek in an hour."

Jefferson Smith was the head of N-Tek, the world's largest manufacturer of extreme-sports equipment. He wasn't Josh's biological father, but Josh's mother, Molly, died when he was only two. Then tragedy struck again two years later when Josh's father, Jim McGrath, died in an avalanche. Since that time, the only family Josh had known was Jefferson Smith, who had adopted his best friend's son.

Josh and Jefferson were close, like a father and son should be, but with Josh studying for his college finals, he had had little free time to spend with his dad.

Josh slipped on a jacket and headed out the door. It would be great to see his dad. Of course, getting a free dinner would be great, too.

Chapter

Beaches. Mountains. Sun. Del Oro Bay was not only a veritable paradise, but home to N-Tek. Josh had spent his entire life in Del Oro Bay. If he wasn't surfing its white-sand beaches, he was snowboarding down white-tipped Mount Corinth. It was the perfect hometown for any extreme-sports nut, and that's exactly what Josh was.

But tonight there was no school, no off-road mountain biking, no exams, just dinner with his dad . . . and a shadowy figure running across the N-Tek grounds.

"What the —" Josh said to himself just as the complex's lights suddenly went out. Josh pulled out his cell phone. Dead. Whatever had knocked out the lights was also affecting his phone.

Josh had been waiting for Jefferson outside N-Tek. Now, he watched the shadowy intruder slip from dark corner to dark corner. *Looks like I'm on my own,* he thought, and chased after the stealthy figure.

Josh hung back in the bushes and watched the intruder kick open the doors to a gardening shed near the rear of the main N-Tek building.

What are you doing? he silently asked, peering through the bushes. *Stealing a lawn mower?*

Josh crept up on the gardening shed. His heart pounded in his chest, as though he had caught a ride on an awesome wave. Josh stopped for a second and felt the rush.

Time to end this, he thought. He flipped around the door and shouted "hey," hoping to surprise the culprit, but the only one who was surprised was Josh.

The shed was empty. The intruder was gone; gone through a hole in the back wall to be exact. Josh looked around the shed. Tools. Garbage cans. The lawn mower was still there. In fact, it looked like everything was still there.

"Why would someone break in here, then kick a hole in the back to sneak out?" Josh wondered.

That was when he saw it. Something metallic reflected from behind the hole in the wall. Josh moved closer. He tugged at the hole, trying to create a space large enough to crawl through. But instead of making the hole bigger, Josh tore down the whole wall! He leapt back and narrowly avoided being smacked by the falling debris.

"I didn't pull it that hard!"

If Josh was shocked that the wall collapsed, he was speechless at what was behind it. An elevator. And it only went one way . . . down into the earth far beneath N-Tek.

Chapter

3

"The wall was a fake," Josh said as he leaned in for a closer inspection. "And why is there an elevator inside a gardening shed?"

As he entered the elevator, Josh wondered how he'd be able to figure out where the intruder had exited, but he quickly realized it didn't matter. There were only two buttons. One said "up," the other "down."

"Why do I feel like Alice?" Josh wondered as he pushed the down button.

The door closed and the elevator dropped. Fast. Josh couldn't tell for sure, but it felt like he was going far beneath the N-Tek headquarters — perhaps a hundred feet or more.

"This better end at the surfboard warehouse," Josh joked, trying to calm himself.

After a few seconds, the elevator slowed, then came to a silent stop. The doors slid open and Josh stepped out.

"Toto, we're not in Del Oro any —"

Two hands grabbed Josh and threw him down. Josh grunted as a knee pushed into his back, pinning him to the ground.

"Who are you?" Josh cried out as two guards pressed his face against the floor and frisked him. "Does Jefferson Smith know you're down here?"

The only answer Josh got was a quick, harsh "shut up."

The two hands lifted Josh to his feet and stood him next to the intruder. Josh glanced up at him. He was huge! His broad shoulders, height, and dark, cold features made him appear more like an evil football player than a surfboard thief — but Josh was beginning to realize this wasn't about stealing N-Tek's new extreme gear.

"I'm probably on your side!" Josh said to the two silent guards as they pushed him and the thief down the corridor. "I was chasing this guy!"

Josh finally gave up and let them lead. The walls were gray steel and doors lined one side. Josh swore that the intruder was . . . counting doors?

"Bingo!" the intruder said and stopped in front of one.

Before Josh could react, the intruder spun and kicked one of the guards in the chest. The second guard went for his weapon, but it was too late. The intruder lifted the guard over his head and threw him at the wall. *Bam!* Both guards slumped to the ground, unconscious.

The intruder swung at Josh, but Josh was ready and dove to the side.

Josh dodged a second swing, but it was just a setup for the third, which landed directly on his chin. Josh collapsed to the floor like a house of cards. Josh knew he was outmatched, so he slumped and pretended to be unconscious.

This guy's really starting to grind on me, Josh thought, waiting for an opening to attack again.

The hulking man kicked in the heavy lab door and entered. Josh crawled over to one of the unconscious guards, grabbed his nightstick, then crept after the intruder.

Once inside, Josh was shocked. High-tech computers were everywhere, video cameras filmed from every corner, and in the center of the room was a giant transparent tank filled with some kind of glowing, bright green fluid.

"What the heck . . ." Josh said aloud.

Josh didn't see him at first, but the intruder heard him. He stood to one side of the giant tank siphoning some of the green fluid into a test tube.

"You're real persistent," the intruder growled, sealing the test tube.

"You bring out my best qualities," Josh quipped.

Josh raised the nightstick over his head and threw it at the intruder, who didn't even have to duck. Josh completely missed him. The intruder turned to watch the nightstick fly by his head.

"At least you hit the wall," the intruder said sarcastically and turned back to Josh . . . just in time to see Josh's right foot before it kicked him in the face.

"Nothing better than a little distraction," Josh said, trying not to smile too much.

Josh spun again to deliver a second roundhouse kick to the intruder's head, but he wasn't so lucky this time. The intruder was fast. In fact he was so fast, he grabbed Josh by the ankle of his kicking foot and lifted his entire body into the air like a rag doll!

Josh was in deep trouble. He squirmed and kicked, but the intruder wouldn't let him go. The alarm finally sounded. Red lights flashed and sirens screamed.

"You're not worth the trouble," the intruder grunted at Josh and threw him against the large tank.

The impact hurt, more than anything Josh had ever felt before. His aches and pains kept telling him to stay down, admit defeat, but Josh would never give up. The nightstick was nearby. Josh grabbed it and forced his aching arm to throw.

Bull's-eye! A direct hit to the head. In fact, the nightstick hit the intruder so hard, it knocked his face off — or at least his mask.

It was gross! The guy's real face was more metal than flesh; his features, cold steel, his eyes, glowing red orbs.

But worst of all, the thing that would haunt Josh's nightmares for months to come was his smile. The lower third of his face formed a giant, metal smile like an evil clown. The image of his insidious grin burned into Josh's mind.

The intruder turned. "You're gonna be real sorry you did that."

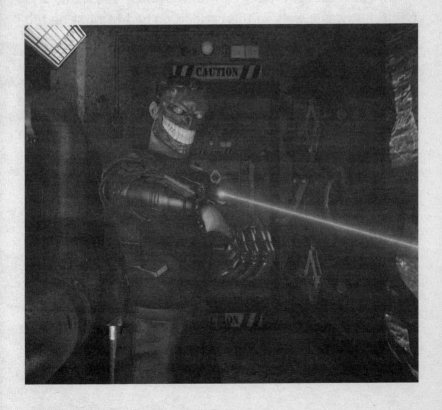

Josh did his best to stand, but it was difficult. His head was foggy and felt like a million kangaroos were hopping across his brain.

The intruder blasted the green tank behind Josh. The glowing green fluid surged out of the tank and flooded over him. There was nothing Josh could do.

If Josh thought being thrown against the tank was painful, it was a walk in the park compared to what he felt now. He gasped for air, then fell to his knees. The green fluid covered his entire body. The last thing he remembered before he blacked out was the strange sensation that the fluid was not only covering him, but going inside of him; through his nose, through his mouth, his ears, his eyes, his *skin*.

Chapter

4

"Josh . . ." the voice said. "Josh?" it repeated.

Josh opened his eyes. Everything was blurry and moved slowly. Josh checked the room. It wasn't the room with the green tank. Where was he?

"Dad?" Josh asked, finally recognizing the voice. "Am I in the hospital?"

"Yes . . . and no. This is N-Tek's private hospital. Everything's going to be fine," Jefferson assured him.

"Why does N-Tek have a hospital? They sell surfboards," Josh questioned.

"We do that, too," Jefferson began. "I think it's time I told you everything N-Tek does."

Josh's dad told him the story, the long story of how N–Tek was formed twenty years ago to fight terrorists worldwide. Josh learned that the extreme-sports products were just a front to hide N-Tek's true mission.

Jefferson went on to tell Josh how the company was the brainchild of Mark Nathanson. Nathanson created N-Tek, Jefferson helped him run it, and Josh's dad, Jim, was their top operative.

"My father was a spy?" Josh gasped.

"One of the best," Jefferson replied.

"So my father . . . the avalanche . . ." Josh asked.

"Is a story better saved for another time," Jefferson continued. "I should have always been honest with you . . . maybe none of this would have happened."

"And what exactly did happen?" Josh asked. "Why do I feel like this? What was that green gunk?"

"That was suspension fluid for something we call 'Nano-Tek Max.'" Jefferson sighed and scratched his goatee. "Microscopic machines capable of reproducing at an astounding rate. There's no limit to what they can do."

"These Max-Probes have invaded your body," Dr. Yevshenko added as she came into the room.

"Machines? *Inside* me? GET 'EM OUT!" Josh yelled.

Dr. Yevshenko lowered her head. "We cannot."

"What'll they do to me?" Josh's voice was panicked.

"We don't know," was all Jefferson could say.

Dr. Yevshenko motioned to Jefferson, gesturing outside where they could speak privately. Jefferson kissed Josh on the forehead and followed the doctor.

"Well . . ." Jefferson asked once he was sure Josh couldn't hear.

"It's only a matter of time," Dr. Yevshenko replied. "The Max-Probes are dying . . . and so is Josh."

Chapter

5

"It's a miracle he even lasted this long," Dr. Yevshenko said, checking Josh's latest blood tests. "His autoimmune system is rejecting the probes."

It had been five days since Josh's accident with the Nano-Tek Max and his condition had only worsened. Jefferson had stood helplessly on the sidelines while they hooked his son to a heart monitor, then an I.V., and finally a respirator. Nothing they had tried had worked and everyone was running out of ideas.

Dr. Yevshenko and Jefferson stood in Josh's room. Josh was unconscious and had been for almost twenty hours.

"So we have to find a way to kill the probes, before they kill Josh?" Jefferson asked.

"We have no other options —"

"There is one," said a young man, coming into the room.

"Who are you?" Jefferson questioned.

"Dr. Roberto Martinez," Dr. Yevshenko acknowledged the newcomer. "'Berto is the new Nano-Tek specialist who just joined N-Tek. I think I told you about him a few days ago . . . ?"

Dr. Yevshenko had said 'Berto Martinez was young, but Jefferson never thought he'd be even younger than Josh. But Jefferson didn't care if he was only eighteen or still wearing diapers; he wanted him to save his son. Jefferson watched the thin, black-haired Colombian make his way to Josh.

'Berto glanced nervously at the others in the room but any apprehension he had left when he saw Josh.

"If the Max-Probes have integrated with his organic systems . . . then the reason he's weakening is that the Probes are literally starving to death."

"What does that mean?" Jefferson quickly asked.

"We shouldn't try to kill the Max-Probes. We need to keep them alive by feeding them," 'Berto continued, pushing his glasses back up his nose. "The Max-Probes need Transphasik Energy to survive. And so does your son. I think."

"It's not that simple," Dr. Yevshenko pointed out. "Transphasik Energy might save Josh — or it might speed the growth of the Probes — killing him that much sooner."

"Do it," a voice said from behind the group. It was Josh.

Jefferson turned. Josh was trying to sit up in bed. Jefferson rushed to his side to help.

"Son, I don't think you realize the risk."

"Look at me, Dad," Josh said, mustering the strength to speak. "I . . . I feel like I'm wasting away. It can't be any worse."

Jefferson turned to Dr. Yevshenko and 'Berto. They all knew this was Josh's decision and none of them could make it for him.

"The man's offering me a chance," Josh weakly added. "Besides . . . he's got Braniac written all over him."

'Berto smiled at the compliment — or at least what he thought was a compliment.

Jefferson and Dr. Yevshenko unhooked Josh from the medical equipment and helped him into a wheelchair. 'Berto grabbed the back and gave Josh a reassuring nod.

'Berto pushed Josh out of his room and the two headed for the Transphasik Energy Chamber.

"Shouldn't you be in elementary school?" Josh asked, trying to be funny.

"Shouldn't you be at the beach?" 'Berto joked back. "I got my Ph.D. when I was seventeen, *hermano*."

"Through the mail?" Josh joked.

They entered the chamber. 'Berto pushed Josh's wheelchair to the center of the room and locked the chair's wheels.

"Fire when ready, bro," Josh said.

"Hang tough, *hermano*. It'll be over soon."

"One way or another."

'Berto retreated from the chamber and joined Jefferson and Dr. Yevshenko behind the protective barrier. 'Berto looked at Jefferson, who gave him the final nod of approval, then hit the power button.

Inside the chamber, Josh was barely able to remain conscious. He heard a loud hum and the floor began to vibrate. Large glass panels lowered, surrounding him on all sides. The vibrations grew and Josh's wheelchair rattled loudly. A spiraling coil hanging from the ceiling hummed to life. Josh looked up just in time to see a warm, golden glow.

"This isn't so bad," he thought.

But then the coil burst to life. A surge of golden light

blasted down on Josh. He felt nothing from the light, but inside his body was a whole different story.

Pain surged through every inch of Josh's being. He screamed out in agony. The vibrating grew louder until Josh couldn't even hear his own painful screams.

From behind the protective barrier, Jefferson could barely watch. He finally grabbed Dr. Yevshenko. "We have to stop this," he pleaded.

"But Jefferson, if Dr. Martinez is right . . ."

It only lasted ten seconds, but to Jefferson it was ten years. Jefferson turned his back on Josh, unable to look.

Finally, 'Berto shut down the power.

"Josh! Josh! Can you hear me?" Jefferson yelled into the microphone.

His worried shouts echoed through the Transphasik Energy Chamber, but Josh didn't reply. In fact, Josh didn't answer, didn't move, didn't breathe.

Chapter

6

Jefferson sat in his office and read a report. There was a terrorist bombing in Berlin and another in London on the same day. There didn't seem to be any link, but that was the last thing on Jefferson's mind right now. He had tried to read the report four times now, but each time just resulted in a headache. Jefferson finally gave up and tossed the report on his desk.

It had become a familiar scene lately: Jefferson too worried to eat, to sleep, to read. And the reason for his concern was always the same. Always Josh.

"Come in," Jefferson said, responding to the knock on his office door.

The door flew open, surprisingly fast considering there was no emergency — at least not today, anyway.

"How was school today?" Jefferson asked the young man standing in the door way.

"Learned all sorts of new tricks," Josh said. "And still a few bugs to work out." Josh held out his hand. Resting in his palm was the doorknob from Jefferson's door.

'Berto had been right. The Max-Probes had been starving. The boost of Transphasik Energy not only saved Josh's life, but the rejuvenated Max-Probes made him faster and stronger, gave him amazing vision, reflexes, and hearing, and other powers that Josh and the N-Tek scientists were only just beginning to discover.

Josh was still Josh, but in some ways he was more than Josh. His personality was the same. He looked the same. He was the same person, but inside, the Max-Probes were evolving, and with them, so was Josh.

With a weekly dose of Transphasik Energy, the Probes would never starve and Josh's potential would be unlimited. The more Josh used his powers, the quicker he needed a recharge of Transphasik Energy, but 'Berto had designed a biolink to monitor Josh's Transphasik Energy levels twenty-four hours a day.

Josh and Jefferson looked at each other and Jefferson smiled. He knew what was coming. It had been three months since the accident and Josh had been in the N-Tek labs all summer training, pushing the limits of his new-found abilities, and honing his skills. Jefferson knew this day would come; he only wished he didn't fear it so much.

"I want to join N-Tek," Josh began.

"Absolutely not!" Jefferson shot back.

"Dad!"

"It's too dangerous, Josh."

"Look, I got these powers for a reason. If it wasn't to

help people, what was it for then? Tell me one person who can do half of what I can."

"You're too young," Jefferson responded.

"I'm older than 'Berto!" Josh countered.

"'Berto . . . Dr. Martinez . . . is a lab rat, not a field operative. Besides, Josh McGrath can't run around the globe battling terrorists and still expect to lead a normal life, go to classes . . . take Laura Chen to the movies."

Laura Chen. Josh's girlfriend. She was away for the summer and had no idea about Josh's accident . . . or his transformation. That was how Josh wanted to keep it. He might be able to bend an iron bar as if it was rubber, but when it came to girls, he still felt like a nervous teenager. And Jefferson was right — fighting terrorists as Josh Mc-Grath would make Laura a target for kidnapping or worse. Josh couldn't put her in that position.

"Okay, Dad. I guess you're right," Josh conceded and slumped his shoulders.

Jefferson smiled. That was easier than he thought it would be. Then Jefferson saw "the look." It was the exact same expression Josh's biological father Jim had worn every time he got a killer idea.

"You're right!" Josh began, perking up. "Josh McGrath can't globe-trot, but *I* can!"

As Josh spoke, he squinted his eyes. A twinkle emanated from his skin and suddenly, Josh's blond hair turned brown, his brown eyes, blue. His jaw widened, his nose became slightly more pointed. Even his shoulders seemed to round out more. Jefferson fell back into his chair, stunned.

"What . . . how . . . what did you . . ." Jefferson stammered.

"I learned how to do this yesterday," Josh excitedly

answered. "It's like this total stealth mode where I tell the Max-Probes to change my appearance to blend with the background. This time, I concentrated on doing something a little different. Now no one will even know I'm Josh McGrath! They'll know me as . . . as . . . Max! Max-Probes!"

Chapter

7

"This is awesome!"

Max flew the small one-man jet, the Hawk, over the German Parliament House in Berlin. Light poured out from the giant glass dome perched atop the building. Max circled once, then opened the Hawk's canopy. He disengaged his shoulder belt, stood in the cockpit, and fired a cable gun down to the radio antenna atop the Parliament House.

Just as quickly as the cable gun's grappling hook snagged the antenna, Max hit the Hawk's autopilot and leaped from the mini-jet.

Using the momentum from the Hawk, Max gripped the cable gun and sailed around the Parliament House like a human kite. Max quickly reeled himself in and came to a rolling stop atop the domed structure.

"Bro, check out the view! I can see the Berlin Wall from up here," Max spoke into his comlink.

Max used the comlink to speak to 'Berto, who had been assigned as Max's base operative. Using the Max-Probes in Josh's body, 'Berto communicated directly to Josh's auditory nerve, so no one but Max — Josh — heard 'Berto's transmissions. 'Berto sat in the newly built Max Room back in the Del Oro N-Tek complex.

The Max Room was created for the sole purpose of monitoring Josh/Max's activities, making sure the Max-Probes in his body were stable, his Transphasik Energy levels high, and everything was smooth sailing.

"Oh, that's right, they did, didn't they?" Max smiled, remembering the Berlin Wall didn't exist anymore. "It's some other wall, then. Patch me in to Rachel."

Jefferson had finally cracked after Josh transformed himself into "Max-Probes." Of course, the first thing that had to happen was a new name. Even Dr. Yevshenko snickered the first time she heard it.

"How about Max Steel," Josh offered after a few moments' thought. No one laughed, so it was a start.

Next came more tests. The more Josh sat in a lab, the more he itched for field action, but each time Jefferson had insisted he "wasn't ready."

One night, when the two of them had gotten together, Josh implored Jefferson to give him — Max — an assignment. Jefferson tried to close the discussion, end the debate before it started, but then Josh said "it."

"I want to carry on Jim McGrath — my dad's work! I want him to be proud of what his son is doing."

If Jefferson had thought the decision to dose Josh with the Transphasik Energy was tough, this was even more difficult. But once again, Jefferson followed Josh's wishes and less than five days later, Max was sent to Berlin with Rachel Leeds to guard the Peace Summit of world ambassadors.

Rachel Leeds was a twenty-six-year-old field operative for N-Tek. Jefferson had referred to her as the "3Bs." British, Beautiful, and the Best. She was an N-Tek espionage expert. Jefferson knew she was a by-the-book professional and had personally picked her to keep an eye on Max.

But right now Max was keeping an eye on her. Even without his improved vision, Max could pick her out from among the other attendees as she walked the Parliament floor.

"Rachel here," Max heard.

"Hey Rach. I'm in position," Max replied.

"Very good, Mr. Steel, but I'm *not* in a position to chat!"

"Look up," Max said, ignoring her complaint.

Rachel did and was shocked to see Max spread-eagled on one of the dome's glass panels.

"Max!" She hissed into her comlink. "You could be seen! What are you thinking?"

"Just taking a little initiative," Max defended. "If I'm sitting in the Hawk when something goes down, I wind up way late for the party."

"As Senior Agent, I am ordering you off that roof," Rachel commanded. "For your own good."

"My own good! What are you, my mother?"

"Think of me as an older sister," Rachel corrected. "With a hammer."

Max watched Rachel work her way across the floor. She looked up once more and shot him a sarcastic sneer.

"You're not sister material, green eyes," Max quipped. "Besides, if I was in charge I would —"

"But you're not in charge," Rachel cut Max off. "Now get off the —"

There was a blinding flash from the room below. The light was so intense, Max rolled back off the glass and covered his eyes. His vision returned after a few seconds.

"'Berto!" Max shouted into his comlink. "They're gone!"

"Who's gone?" 'Berto responded.

"Everybody."

Max looked down into the Parliament Building. Where only seconds before the floor had been crowded with Rachel and hundreds of ambassadors, there now was emptiness as ominous as a dark storm cloud blotting the sun from the clear blue sky.

Chapter

8

"Keep your head steady, Max. And don't blink!"

'Berto used the Max-Probes in Max's eyes to scan the Parliament floor. Nothing.

"I'll call your dad," 'Berto said to Max.

"And what am I supposed to do?"

"Uh . . . wait?"

"Uh . . . no," Max replied and raised his fist.

"Max! No!" 'Berto yelled through the comlink, but it was too late. 'Berto watched on the giant monitor before him as Max's fist smashed through the window.

Max locked a grappling hook to the dome and rappeled to the floor below. The view looked the same inside the building as it did from above the building: empty. Max walked around, having no real clue what to search for.

"Where is everybody?! Who are you?!" a voice called out from behind Max.

Max spun around to see the young attaché race from the room shouting, "Security!"

"I guess he's even more surprised than me," Max thought.

Max knew the attaché would be coming back in seconds with a fleet of armed men, which was exactly what he didn't need right then.

Max concentrated and the colors of his skin, hair, and bodysuit instantly changed to match the wallpaper behind him.

"I love stealth mode," Max smiled as he practically disappeared. "Austin Powers, eat your heart out!"

Max had pulled his invisible man act just in time. Seconds later the attaché returned with a small band of armed guards.

"Where is everybody?" one guard called out.

"Impossible!" cried another.

"Sound the alarm!"

"We have an intruder!"

"Shut down all the exits!"

The attaché walked around the large room searching for Max. The guards followed suit, but no one thought to look at the empty wall, and if they had, they would've seen a figure, one that looked like the wallpaper itself, slip under a table.

Max checked his surroundings and changed his wallpaper appearance to an oak camouflage to match the floor.

"Bring me up to speed," Max heard boom through his head.

"Not so loud!" Max hissed back.

"Can they hear me?" Jefferson asked, slightly panicked. He had joined 'Berto in the Max Room after hearing the news. "I thought this broadcast directly into your head."

"It does!" Max reassured him. "But you've got the volume cranked!"

Jefferson smiled at 'Berto and slid the volume toggle down. "Sorry, son," Jefferson sheepishly added.

"There's nothing here, boss. No Rachel, no briefcases, no coffee cups, no pens. Hey . . . are the chairs supposed to be bolted to the floor?"

"Bolted?" 'Berto questioned. "*Hermano*, focus on one of the long conference tables."

Max poked his head over the top of the table and zoomed in on the top of another one.

Back in the Del Oro Max Room, 'Berto received the transmission and computer-analyzed the image.

"Computer enhancements reveal no fingerprints," he announced.

"Am I supposed to believe that everyone in that room was wearing gloves?" Jefferson asked.

"Wearing gloves . . . or they were never even *in* this room," Max added.

Before Jefferson or 'Berto could respond, a red light flashed on the Max Room's control panel.

"What is that?" Jefferson asked urgently. "Is Josh — I mean Max okay?!"

"He's fine, sir," 'Berto reassured him. "That's just an incoming priority message."

"Good. Put it in the monitor and patch it through to Max."

'Berto pushed the red button and N-Tek agent Mairot appeared on the screen.

"Sir," Mairot began immediately. "We've just got word that a terrorist named 'L'Étranger' has claimed responsibility for the abductions. He's asking a million American dollars . . ."

"That's not so bad," 'Berto replied.

"Per head!" Mairot clarified. "He's given the German government four hours before he starts to —"

"I understand," Jefferson said to Mairot. "Search the files for any other activity on this L'Étranger. Contact us immediately if you find anything."

"Understood, sir. Mairot out."

"That brain of yours come up with anything yet?" Jefferson asked 'Berto as Mairot's image faded from the monitor. "L'Étranger just put a clock on this."

"It's a long shot, but check this out. I'm guessing the Parliament floor rotated 180 degrees, sending Rachel and the diplomats into a hidden chamber, while a new floor spun into place. The flash was used to blind any security cameras!"

As 'Berto described his theory to Jefferson, the computer hummed to life and created a simulation of the entire Parliament floor rotating, sending the ambassadors and Rachel into the basement while a fake floor rotated into place.

"Good work, Dr. Martinez," Jefferson praised. "I've got another N-Tek team in trouble in Belfast. You both seem to have the situation under control . . ."

"We do?" 'Berto questioned.

Jefferson didn't respond. He simply turned and walked out of the Max Room. Once out of the room, Jefferson took a deep breath and crossed his fingers. "Be safe, Josh. Be safe," he whispered to himself.

"Uh . . . what just happened?" Max asked 'Berto.

"Boss put you in charge."

"Me?!" Max practically shouted into his comlink, forgetting for an instant that he was still hiding from security. "He's way gone, bro! I've been a secret agent for less than three months! This is my first field mission! I can't be in charge!"

"You've been complaining about calling the shots since I met you," Max heard in his head.

"I'm nineteen, Einstein!" Max yelped back. "I'm *supposed* to complain and the big chief is *supposed* to ignore me."

Another security patrol headed down the hall. Max checked his stealth mode to make sure he matched the walls.

"You can't stay in stealth mode forever," 'Berto warned him. "You'll run out of energy soon."

"I know!" Max whispered. "Shh. Here they come."

The three guards walked down the hall. Their weapons were holstered, which was good, but it would be a tight squeeze for Max to slip by in the narrow hall. Max stood and slid carefully along the wall as the guards walked by, completely unaware of his presence.

That was close, Max thought.

And it got even closer once Max's biolink started to ring like a phone.

"What's that?! What's that?!" Max heard 'Berto yelling in his head. "Why is it ringing?!"

The guards heard the ringing, too. They spun around and drew their weapons.

"Don't move or we'll shoot!" one yelled.

Chapter

9

Max froze. The guards couldn't see him, but they could hear him — or at least his ringing comlink. Max quickly disconnected the incoming transmission and the ringing stopped, but the guards continued to creep forward, all three pointing their guns directly at him.

"I heard ringing," one guard said.

"It came from here," another responded.

Max didn't wait around to hear what the third guard would say. He slowly moved away until he reached an intersection, then ran down the hall and into a bathroom.

The comlink rang again.

"What is that?" 'Berto's voice was frustrated.

"Hello?" Max said, pressing the channel button on his comlink.

"Hello?" a female voice replied.

"Rachel?!" Max enthused.

"Rachel? Josh, who's Rachel?"

"Laura? Is that you?" Max asked, realizing the voice belonged to his girlfriend, Laura Chen.

Laura had decided to spend the summer traveling through her homeland of China. At first Josh had been unhappy at the thought of her being gone for so long — until the accident. Then he realized that Laura's absence would be the perfect time for Josh to take a vacation, too — and for Max Steel to have a full summer of training.

"Laura! I've missed you," Max continued. "This was the worst summer ever! Way too long to be apart!"

"Who's Rachel?" Laura shot back, completely ignoring Max's enthusiasm.

"Rachel . . . didn't I write about her?" Max began, trying to cover. "She's the old lady handling publicity for the Del Oro Extreme."

"I thought her name was Margaret."

Max flinched. "Yeah . . . Margaret's her . . . last name."

"Rachel Margaret?"

"Yeah," Max replied. The phone was silent. Max waited to see if his lame cover-up worked.

"Sorry," Laura began and thought she heard a sigh of relief from Max. "I guess I forgot. Three months *is* way too long. That's why I called. I'm coming home!"

A man came in to use the bathroom and Max moved into a stall.

"That's great," he whispered into the comlink.

"Why are you whispering?"

"I'm not," Max whispered. "Overseas phone call. You know . . ."

Max watched the man wash his hands and check his hair in the mirror. The man pulled a paper towel from the dispenser, then suddenly stopped. He turned toward Max's stall and tilted his head, as if he was listening.

"Can you pick me up at the airport?"

Max didn't respond. He watched the man shake his head, pause for a moment, then turn to the bathroom door.

"Josh . . . ?"

"Yeah, sorry! You dropped out for a second," Max lied.

"So, tomorrow, seven A.M.?"

"Tomorrow!?" Max's surprise got the best of him again.

"I'm so excited to see you!" Laura enthused. "My plane's boarding. Gotta go!"

The moment Max heard Laura hang up the phone, 'Berto's voice filled his head.

"Let me guess: you forwarded your home phone to your comlink so you wouldn't miss any personal calls?"

"Seemed like a good idea at the time," Max defended.

Chapter

10

Max had worked his way to the Parliament's boiler room. 'Berto figured that if Max was going to be punching holes in walls trying to find the secret room, it would be best to start where no one would see him.

"What's the plan 'Berto?" Max asked after making sure the boiler room was empty.

"I don't know. I guess just start punching holes in the walls until you find a passage."

"That's not a plan, bro, that's carnage."

"Are you complaining?"

"No way," Max said and balled his fist. "Going turbo!"

Although it was a great drain on his power supply, Max loved "going turbo." When he did, he practically became superhuman. "It makes me feel like Superman," Max had said. "Without the cape."

Max punched the wall across from the entry. The concrete exploded outward from the impact, revealing a second room.

"Would you look at that," Max said, surprised he got it on the first punch.

Max stepped through the hole in the wall. Light filtered

in from the boiler room and what he saw amazed him. On the ceiling of the dark room Max had just entered was an exact duplicate of the Parliament floor.

"You were right, bro. They flipped the whole dang room over!"

"I've got a lock on Rachel!" 'Berto excitedly told Max. "That wall must've been blocking her signal!"

"Point the way!"

'Berto downloaded the coordinates into Max's comlink and he was off. Max raced across the duplicate room and kicked in a door at the far end. In front of him was a long, dark corridor.

"Keep pushing, *hermano*. We've got two more hours before L'Étranger starts harming the hostages."

"Trust me, I won't give him the chance."

Max ran down another corridor, then another and another until he felt like he was a rat racing through a giant maze. Finally, the twisting passages opened to a secret entrance into the Berlin subway system. Max rushed onto the subway platform just as a train pulled away.

"Quick!" 'Berto yelled. "Tag the train with a tracer and wait for backup!"

"No way," Max replied. "We're doing this . . . the Max Steel way!"

Max ignored 'Berto's protests and raced across the platform. He leaped off the edge, did a full somersault, and sailed toward the last train. Max hit the top and rolled over twice from the momentum, but it carried him across the train car and off the other side. At the last instant, Max grabbed the top of the train and saved himself. The wall sped by inches from Max's head. Max's heart pounded in his chest. One false move and Max Steel would be Max Pancake.

Max waited a few seconds until the tunnel widened, then pulled himself up. He took a deep breath and calmed.

"That was too close," he said to himself and peered over the edge.

"And this will be even closer," a voice behind him boasted.

Max spun. L'Étranger stood directly in front of him. He was bigger than Max by at least six inches. L'Étranger wore black body armor and a tight, black mesh mask that made his face look like a skeleton head. Before Max could react, L'Étranger delivered a roundhouse kick to Max's head.

"Last one on, first one off," L'Étranger joked as his heel landed on Max's jaw. Max staggered backward. The train accelerated and Max never had a chance.

He stumbled backward off the end of the train and fell into the darkness. The train sped away without him.

"Max! Max!" 'Berto screamed into his microphone. "Answer me, Max! Are you okay? MAX!"

But no matter how loud 'Berto yelled, the only response he heard was the low hiss of emptiness.

Chapter

'Berto nervously scanned the control panel. Should he call Jefferson? No. He had to solve this on his own. He took a deep breath. Max was unconscious. What could he do to help from half a world away?

"Guess I just wait until he comes to," 'Berto figured.

That was when he heard it. It was coming through Max's comlink. It was a low rattling at first, but it grew louder and louder with each second.

"Oh no!" 'Berto realized. "It's another train! And Max is lying on the tracks! Wake up, *hermano*! WAKE UP!"

'Berto quickly discerned that yelling into the comlink was a waste of time, but what alternative did he have?

"Think, genius. Think!" 'Berto wracked his brain. "Comlink feedback!" finally burst from his mouth.

The oncoming train was louder. 'Berto had no time to spare. He quickly hit a few buttons and sent a biolink feedback pulse directly into Max's head.

"Ow!" Max yelled as the loud whine stabbed into his head. "What'd you do to me?"

"Jump, Max! Jump!"

Max didn't need to ask why. He heard the subway train

horn blaring behind him as he jumped to the far set of tracks. The trained zoomed by, barely missing Max.

"What happened?" Max asked after the train passed.

"I had to wake you up. Did it hurt much?"

"Just send me a bottle of aspirin." Max eyed the tracks. "Where's the train with Rachel?"

"Long gone, *hermano*."

"I'm a total crash and burn," Max groaned. He pounded his fist into his palm, then punched the wall.

"Max . . ."

"No! This isn't one of your chess problems! L'Étranger knows we're on to him! If he finds out who Rachel is . . ."

"He hasn't yet," 'Berto assured him.

"He will! This is whacked! I can't be in charge!" Max yelled into his comlink. "If something happens to Rachel because of me . . ."

Max slumped against the wall. He had never felt so helpless, so completely useless. Maybe Josh was wrong. Maybe he wasn't cut out to be an N-Tek agent. It didn't matter how much power or strength he had, if he didn't start thinking, Rachel was a goner.

"I'm sending help," 'Berto finally said.

The next thing Max knew, something blasted a hole in the subway ceiling and showered him with rubble.

"Dude, exactly what kind of help did you have in mind?" Max asked as he dove clear of the rubble.

The Hawk hovered over the newly made hole. From the bottom of the Hawk, a small, sleek jet-luge disengaged and flew down to Max.

"The Sparrow!" Max's mood brightened once he realized he had a way to chase L'Étranger. "'Berto, you are extreme! Locked onto Rachel's signal. We're go!"

Max leaped onto the Sparrow and locked himself in. He flicked two switches and the jet-luge fired its mini-rockets. It zoomed down the subway tunnel and was devoured by the darkness.

Chapter

12

The train rattled down the tracks. Rachel sat quietly with the other ambassadors, knowing that Max would be there any minute. The only real question she had was what would Max do once he *did* get there? Each train had armed guards, dressed in black Kevlar body armor.

The door opened up. Rachel tilted her head to see L'Étranger enter. Most of the ambassadors kept their heads down, not wanting to make eye contact.

"I'm afraid my manners have been atrocious; I neglected to introduce myself," L'Étranger began. "People call me L'Étranger."

"The Stranger?" Rachel commented, translating from French.

L'Étranger smiled. He walked over to Rachel and stood over her. "To everyone but you, I hope."

L'Étranger reached for Rachel's hand. She tried to pull it back, but he lifted it to his mouth and gave it a gentle kiss.

"It would be a shame if *something* should happen to someone as beautiful as you. And if my ransom is not paid within one hour, something *will*."

While L'Étranger acquainted himself with his hostages, Max closed in. The Sparrow was running low on fuel, but Max was practically on top of the speeding train.

"Matching speed."

"What are you going to do?" 'Berto asked.

"Take charge." Max stood up on the Sparrow and gained his balance. "Grab the wheel, bro — I'm outta here!"

Max jumped from the Sparrow to the train. For the second time, he landed atop the rolling metal snake, and this time he did it with ease.

Max crept to the edge of the train, leaned over, and peered into the window of the number-five car. Several terrorists occupied the car, but no L'Étranger. Rachel, the ambassadors, and two more terrorist guards were in the number-four car.

"Go through the back, take out the guards, detach the train . . ." Max readied himself.

Just as he was about to make his move, his comlink rang again. Max punched the receive button.

"Hey, Laura."

"How'd you know it was me," Laura's voice sounded in Max's head.

"A guy can dream," Max replied and slowly crept across the train.

"I can barely hear you? What's —"

"I unforwarded your calls," 'Berto cut in. "No more interruptions."

"When she gets home, I am such dead meat," Max lamented.

Max jumped from the top of the last subway car to the connecting platform between it and the next car.

"Going turbo," Max reported.

A charge of golden energy pulsed through his body. Max reached down to the connecting pin and snapped it in half. The two train cars disconnected. Separated from the engine, the fifth car slowed and came to a stop.

"Get some authorities after those guys," Max said to 'Berto, then turned to sneak a peek into the number-four car.

Max signaled Rachel. She smiled and nodded just as one of the armored terrorists noticed the last subway car was gone. The terrorist ran to the back door. He slammed it open. Max's grabbing hand greeted him.

Max knew the body armor would protect the terrorist, so he pulled him from the train and flung him over the side.

The second terrorist went for her shock-stick. Too late. Rachel kicked her stomach, grabbed the dropped shock-stick, and gave the terrorist a healthy jolt of electricity. The terrorist slumped to the floor unconscious.

Max casually walked to Rachel and smiled.

"Miss me?" he asked.

Chapter

13

"Do I look like a terrorist?" Rachel asked Max.

The body armor was a tight fit, but she didn't have much choice. The protective helmet covered her face, which would allow her to work her way through the subway cars unmolested and sweep up any remaining terrorists.

Meanwhile, Max was back on the train's roof. It was his mission to detach the engine car from the rest of the train cars and stop the whole production. Max worked his way to the engine car, where two terrorists stood on guard.

Max jumped down, taking them by surprise. He punched one square in the jaw. The man smashed through the door of the number-two car and sailed half its length before landing in a heap.

The second terrorist grabbed his shock-stick and gave Max a hefty zap. It would have knocked any normal man unconscious, but since when was Max Steel a normal man? It did hurt. Badly. But Max fought the blackness growing in his head and grabbed the stick, snapping it in half.

Max fell to one knee. The terrorist pulled out a club. Max readied himself for the blow, but the terrorist fell over instead. Rachel stood behind him, holding her own shock-stick.

"Miss me?" Rachel smirked.

"So I guess it went well?"

"There were two more in the car behind this one. Let's just say they'll be dozing for awhile."

Max kneeled to the connector pin and snapped it in half. He and Rachel stood on the platform of the number-two car and watched the train's engine pull away. L'Étranger was still on the engine car and had no idea his plan had failed.

"That ends that," Rachel said.

"Not quite," Max said.

Without another word, he leaped to the engine car. Rachel was helpless to stop him.

"Sorry, Rach," he yelled as the number-two car rolled to a stop. "I've got a score to settle!"

The engine car's back door slammed open. It was L'Étranger. He cursed under his breath, realizing he had been cut off from his hostages.

"Lose something?" a voice said from above him.

L'Étranger looked to the top of the engine car. Max sat; his feet dangling over the edge.

"I suppose I have you to thank?" L'Étranger sneered.

"A team effort," Max shrugged. "But yeah . . . mostly me."

"And now you've stayed to . . . even the score?"

"I'm so glad you know the rules," Max wisecracked.

Max prepared himself. L'Étranger climbed the ladder and stared Max down. Both men were silent. The rattling subway train echoed around them, but neither one moved. Each waited . . . for an opening . . . a weakness . . . a . . .

Max lunged first, but L'Étranger stopped his swing cold by grabbing his wrist. L'Étranger squeezed and Max could swear he heard something crack.

Max swept a leg, knocking L'Étranger's feet from under him. L'Étranger flopped to his back. Max rolled away and checked his wrist. Nothing broken. Yet.

The train sped along. Max and L'Étranger sized up each other once more. Both men waited for the other to move first. Suddenly Max noticed that L'Étranger was about to duck. He spun, just in time to see a low ceiling beam zoom his way. Max rolled again, narrowly avoiding being pummeled by the beam. The moment they were clear, L'Étranger was on him.

L'Étranger leaped in the air and came down with his knee. Max rolled to the side. L'Étranger's knee punctured a hole in the train's roof.

"This guy means business," Max heard 'Berto say.

"So do I, bro," Max countered.

Before Max could stand, L'Étranger came at him again with another kick. Once more, Max dodged, but the rocking train pushed him too far to the side and Max rolled off the edge.

"Déjà vu!" Max thought as he grabbed the side.

L'Étranger moved in for the kill. Max hit turbo. His arms basked in the familiar golden glow. Max quickly pulled himself back to the car roof before L'Étranger could stop him.

"Let's try that once more!" Max called out.

Max and L'Étranger both charged. They countered each other's punches and grappled on the racing train. Max was still in turbo mode, but he couldn't throw L'Étranger!

"You . . . can't be that strong!" Max grunted.

"Stranger yet, neither can you!" L'Étranger spat.

Both fighters broke their grips and each delivered a series of quick judo blows. Then L'Étranger broke through with a double palm-thrust to Max's chest. Max reeled backward and nearly went over the edge again!

"I'm open to suggestions!" Max called to 'Berto.

"I suggest you get the heck outta there! Bite his kneecaps off! Anything!" 'Berto hastily stammered.

"Kneecaps, you say? That gives me an idea," Max

replied and hit the turbo button on his comlink. Max pushed a second button and focused the golden energy in his legs only.

L'Étranger closed the distance, preparing his final blow for Max. Max backed up. L'Étranger moved closer. Max backed away, to the very edge of the train.

"Going somewhere?" L'Étranger scoffed.

"No, but you are!"

Max flopped onto his back. Faster than he had ever moved before, Max delivered a turbo-powered kick to the legs of L'Étranger. The blow caught L'Étranger off guard and sent him reeling backward.

Max didn't hesitate, he leaped to his feet and delivered a second turbo kick to the chest of the off-balance L'Étranger. L'Étranger flew backward and off the back end of the train. Max watched as L'Étranger grew smaller and smaller as the train sped down the track.

Chapter

14

"Rachel's okay and the German authorities have all the hostages and nearly all the terrorists in custody," 'Berto told Max.

"Nearly?"

"There's no sign of L'Étranger."

"Figures," Max sighed.

Max guided the Sparrow to rendezvous back with the Hawk. He was exhausted. The only thing he wanted more than sleep was food.

"Max? This is Jefferson." Max heard Jefferson's voice come in through his comlink.

"Hey . . . boss," Max replied.

"'Berto tells me you did all right."

"I earned my allowance," Max said, hoping his dad would agree.

"Next time, maybe you can just clean your room?" Jefferson joked.

"Dare to dream, but I wouldn't hold my breath," Max laughed back.

"I'm not," Jefferson conceded. "So . . . L'Étranger . . . escaped?"

Max punched the Hawk's dash. Did Jefferson have to remind him that L'Étranger had escaped? Max shook his head and ran his fingers through his hair.

"We don't know," Max sighed. "Probably. Look, I blew it, okay? I'm sorry."

Jefferson sensed the anger in Max's voice. "Calm down, Josh. I'm not trying to —"

"I am calm!" Max snapped back. "And I'll get the creep next time!"

"I just wanted to —"

But Max was in no mood to listen. He was angry that L'Étranger had escaped and nothing Jefferson said would change that.

"I'm hittin' major turbulence up here," Max said, cutting off Jefferson. "We'll talk later, okay, Dad? Steel out."

Max flicked off the comlink. He put the Hawk on autopilot and stared out the window. Next time he would do better, Max told himself. Next time it would be different. Next time . . .

Below him, the ocean surged and swayed, indifferent to Max's anguish. The Hawk zoomed over the uncaring sea and into the face of the setting sun.

The haunting figure sat alone in the dark. He awaited news. It had only been four hours, but it felt like four days.

Had the money transfer been made? Why hadn't L'Étranger reported yet?

There were so many more plans relying on the success of this one. It would be the first in a long scheme to global destabilization, conquest, and domination. Domination for Dread.

But the best plans start small, quiet. And this would be his beginning.

The door cracked open. A beam of light cut through the room and fell on Dread. He looked at the messenger standing in the doorway.

"L'Étranger failed," was all the messenger said.

Rage boiled under his skin, but Dread contained it. It was foolish to show the cracks in his cool demeanor before a mere messenger.

"N-Tek, I suppose," Dread hissed.

The messenger nodded.

"N-Tek has become quite the thorn in my side. It is time to remove it."

This was a setback for Dread, but there had been others and this would not be the last. Of course, all that would change once he killed Jefferson Smith.

Josh raced the car down the Del Oro coast. Laura's plane would be landing in five minutes. He popped a sugar doughnut in his mouth, floored the accelerator, and zoomed toward the airport.

Once there, he checked himself in the mirror to make sure he looked just right for Laura. Good thing. Josh was still in his Max Steel identity. Josh looked around to make sure no one was nearby, then with a moment of concentration, his features shimmered with golden energy. Brown hair morphed to blond, blue eyes to brown.

"Hello, stranger," Josh said, seeing his real appearance in the rearview mirror.

"Finally!" Josh heard a voice call out.

He hopped out of the car and ran up to Laura, who had just come out of the airport main door.

"Sorry, sorry, sorry, sorry I'm so late!"

"I thought you were going to meet me at the gate," Laura chided.

"I . . . overslept," Josh sheepishly fibbed. He reached into his bag of doughnuts and pulled out a jelly-filled. "But I brought doughnuts . . ."

"I'd rather have you," Laura responded.

Laura dropped her luggage and threw her arms around Josh. They hugged tightly.

After several minutes, they finally pulled away. Josh gazed into Laura's beautiful brown eyes. He twisted her black hair with one of his fingers.

"I missed you," he offered.

"Me, too. Now what have you been up to all summer?" Laura quizzed.

Josh smiled. It was a smile of arrival — the kind of smile when everything is finally okay after a long battle. And it had been a long battle, from the mysterious intruder, to the green liquid, to near death, to training, to L'Étranger. But now it all seemed like a dream.

"Oh, same old, same old," Josh laughed.